A Summery Saturday Morning

To Alice and Poppy—the goose-and-dog girls.
—M.M.
For my mum.
—S.Y.

PUFFIN BOOKS
Published by the Penguin Group
Penguin Putnam Books for Young Readers, 345 Hudson Street, New York, New York 10014, U.S.A.
Penguin Books Ltd, 27 Wrights Lane, London W8 5TZ, England
Penguin Books Australia Ltd, Ringwood, Victoria, Australia
Penguin Books Canada Ltd, 10 Alcorn Avenue, Toronto, Ontario, Canada M4V 3B2
Penguin Books (N.Z.) Ltd, 182-190 Wairau Road, Auckland 10, New Zealand

Penguin Books Ltd, Registered Offices: Harmondsworth, Middlesex, England

First published in Great Britain by Hamish Hamilton Ltd, 1998
First published in the United States of America by Viking, a member of Penguin Putnam Inc., 1998
Published by Puffin Books, a member of Penguin Putnam Books for Young Readers, 2000

A Vanessa Hamilton Book

1 3 5 7 9 10 8 6 4 2

Text copyright © Margaret Mahy, 1998
Illustrations copyright © Selina Young, 1998
All rights reserved

THE LIBRARY OF CONGRESS HAS CATALOGED THE VIKING EDITION UNDER CATALOG CARD NUMBER: 97-61542

Puffin Books ISBN 0-14-056720-8

Printed in China

Margaret Mahy

A Summery Saturday Morning

Illustrated by Selina Young

PUFFIN BOOKS

We take the dogs down the wiggly track,
The wiggly track, the wiggly track.
One dog's white and the other dog's black
On a summery Saturday morning.

Bad dogs, bad dogs chase the cat,
Chase the cat, chase the cat.
One dog's thin and the other dog's fat
On a summery Saturday morning.

They chase the boy on the rattly bike,
The rattly bike, the rattly bike.
Chasing things is what dogs like
On a summery Saturday morning.

Long grass grows on the edge of the sea,
The edge of the sea, the edge of the sea.
The wind is blowing wild and free
On a summery Saturday morning.

A goose looks out of the tangled green,
The tangled green, the tangled green.
Her neck is long and her eye is mean
On a summery Saturday morning.

Another goose ... and then another,
Then another, then another!
Seven sleek sisters out with mother
On a summery Saturday morning.

The geese begin to run away,
Run away, run away.
The dogs run, too. They want to play
On a summery Saturday morning.

We run, too, to catch the dogs,
To catch the dogs, to catch the dogs –
Scattering shells and leaping logs
On a summery Saturday morning.

The mud begins its guggliwugs,
Its guggliwugs, its guggliwugs.
Our sandals slide like slugliwugs
On a summery Saturday morning.

The geese turn round and flap and hiss,
Flap and hiss, flap and hiss.
The dogs were not expecting this
On a summery Saturday morning.

The geese begin to chase us back,
To chase us back, to chase us back.
Out of the mud and up the track
On a summery Saturday morning.

If you want to walk in peace,
Walk in peace, walk in peace,
Don't let your dogs upset the geese
On a summery Saturday morning.

Margaret Mahy is a versatile and world-renowned storyteller with more than one hundred children's books to her credit. She has won the Carnegie Medal twice, and in 1993 she was awarded her country's most prestigious honor, the Order of New Zealand. Among Ms. Mahy's most recent picture books are *Beaten by a Balloon*, illustrated by Jonathan Allen, and *Boom, Baby, Boom, Boom!*, illustrated by Patricia MacCarthy. Ms. Mahy lives in Lyttelton, New Zealand.

Although **Selina Young** has illustrated more than a dozen books for children, this is her first collaboration with a fellow New Zealander. Ms. Young also lives in Lyttelton, New Zealand.